Ruby Red Shoes
Goes to Paris

KATE KNAPP

MACMILLAN CHILDREN'S BOOKS

First published in Australia 2013 by Angus & Robertson, an imprint of
HarperCollins*Publishers* Australia Pty Limited

First published in the UK 2018 by Macmillan Children's Books
an imprint of Pan Macmillan
20 New Wharf Road, London N1 9RR
Associated companies throughout the world
www.panmacmillan.com

ISBN 978-1-5098-9287-7

1 3 5 7 9 8 6 4 2

A CIP catalogue record for this book is available from
the British Library.

Cover and internal design by Natalie Winter
The illustrations in this book were created in pencil and watercolour
Colour reproduction by Graphic Print Group, Adelaide
Printed and bound in China

For my beloved sister Samantha

Ruby Red Shoes is a white hare who
lives in a prettily painted caravan with her
grandmother Babushka Galina Galushka.

Ruby Red Shoes and her grandmother are going
on a holiday and the first city they are visiting is Paris.
Ruby is fizzing with excitement.

Ruby's chickens are a little upset that they're not also
going to Paris. They have been studying French with
great determination and have even given themselves
new French names. But they're happy for Ruby and
sing out 'au revoir' with impeccable French accents.

The airport is busy when Ruby and
her grandmother arrive.

They have their tickets.
They have their passports.
They have their luggage.

The Flying Hare

And they are taking off with their
favourite airline – The Flying Hare.

Ruby can't quite believe how high
they are flying. Higher than the clouds
and close to her beloved stars.

Babushka and Ruby
arrive in Paris and
zip along the streets in
a taxi to where they
are staying.

Their apartment is on the top floor.
A rattling lift takes them some of the way,
then they climb up a narrow, twirling staircase
to their rooms at the top of the building.

Babushka struggles
with the old keys and
creaky lock but soon
they're inside.

At first the rooms seem dark and full of shadows.
It's very different from their cosy caravan.
But Babushka knows how to make things brighter.
Within moments she has turned on lamps,
found the teapot and is warming some soup.
Everything starts to feel homely and rather exciting.

Ruby looks from their balcony to the square below.
There are small tables arranged underneath colourful awnings.
Warm lights glow from all the windows.

Ruby loves the forest of terracotta chimneys growing all
over the slate rooftops. Then in a window across the square,
Ruby spots a friendly face and they wave shyly at each other.

Ruby's red shoes are twitching to go out
and explore, but Babushka Galushka says it's
dusk-o'clock and that her shoes will have to be
patient and get a good night's sleep first.

The sun is barely awake when Ruby
sleepily opens one eye and hears the song
of Paris wafting in through the window.

It's a chorus of tooting scooters, bicycle bells, delivery
trucks inching down narrow laneways, ladies' shoes
clipping on cobblestones and a harmony of delicate
chinks as coffee cups kiss their saucers.

They head off to the local market.
Ruby's shoes are so aflutter to be
going out she has to try with all her
might to keep them from bolting.

She imagines them like spirited horses
she reins in with her shoelaces.

The market is bustling, and there is so much interesting
and beautiful food, Ruby doesn't know where to look.

The plump red raspberries catch
her eye first,

then the red speckled strawberries,

the rosy red apples,

and the shiny red
redcurrants!

There are cheeses of every description,
eggs of every colour, and breads of every shape.
There is butter from every corner of France,
and jams of every possible fruit.

And every pastry is perfect.

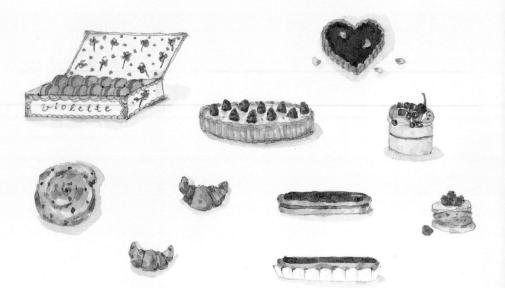

There are crêpes
with every delicious
filling and flavour.

Sucre
Citron
Chocolat
Miel

After shopping they meet Babushka Galushka's brother
Monsieur Gaspar Galushka, who lives in an apartment
above his hat shop. He loves hats as much as Ruby
loves red shoes. And with Great Uncle Gaspar is his
grandson Felix. The boy Ruby had waved to!

When Babushka Galushka and Gaspar catch up
later in the afternoon, Felix and Ruby head off on
racy scooters to beetle around the city together.

Ruby has tucked her new travel notebook
and coloured pencils into her satchel.

Over the next few days,

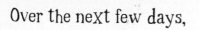

they see,

hear,

feel,

smell

and taste

Paris!

In her notebook, Ruby records what she sees.

The
Eiffel
Tower

If I were a statue ...

I'd have a radish on my nose

and I'd have baguettes for ears!

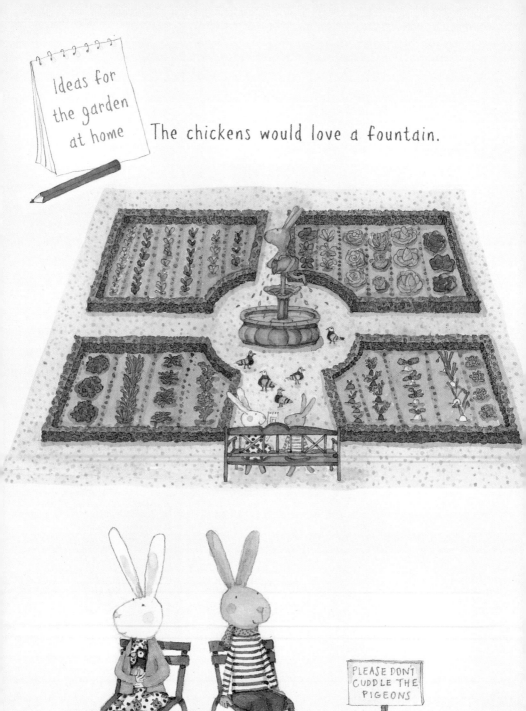

Ideas for the garden at home

The chickens would love a fountain.

PLEASE DON'T CUDDLE THE PIGEONS

Lovely signs.

The prettiest, most
ornate doors I've
ever seen. Perhaps
a new door for the
chickens' house?

It's me. I'm a tree!

The Paris
Flower
Markets

My bees would love it here.

Croissant Smiles.

Dear Chickens,
Bonjour from Paris!
Having a great time.
Wish you were here.
Missing you.
Love Ruby xxx

My Chickens
1 Carrot Lane
Home

Dear Chickens,
I have learnt that
the Rooster is a
symbol of France.
Love Ruby xxx

My Chickens
1 Carrot Lane
Home

Postcards home!

Dear Chickens,
I found the breadcrumbs
you'd put in my socks
just in case I was hungry!
Thanks for the thought
but there is plenty to
eat in Paris.
Love Ruby xxx

My Chickens
1 Carrot Lane
Home

POSTES

There is lots of love in Paris.

One day they stop to buy buttered baguettes
and huge peaches. The taste of the creamy butter,
warm bread and fragrant fruit makes Ruby light-headed.
She soon drifts off, imagining her chickens in Paris
with her, savouring the local food. It's quite a nice
dream until she sees what they order!

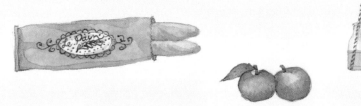

Escargots ... snails!

On Ruby's last day, they climb up the steep
hill to visit the church of Sacré-Cœur, which
sits like an angel watching over Paris.

They tiptoe inside and sit silently.
The blinking candles and glorious voices of
the singing nuns give them goosebumps.

In that moment their hearts are full.
Grateful for all they've seen, for friends,
for family and for being together.

Once outside, they notice the sun has
almost gone to bed so they skip down a
stream of steps, just in time for a farewell
dinner with their grandparents.

They are dining at Café de Flore, famous as a meeting place for poets, philosophers, writers and artists. They order pommes frites - chips! - and croquemadame, which is delicious egg and cheese on toast.

Then after a silky hot chocolate Felix announces he has written Ruby a farewell poem. He would like to read it to her.

There was a white hare from far away,

Who came to Paris for a holiday.

Never without red shoes on her feet,

She scooted with me along many a street.

We found the dottiest of dots,

We liked the spottiest of spots.

We found every flavour of jam to spread,

On our crispy, crunchy, beautiful bread.

We saw stripes up and down and all over town,

On shirts, on tights from reds to whites.

We looked at and noted every shade of red,

The fire-truck kind was your favourite, you said.

My cousin, my friend, I wish this visit would never end.

Dear Ruby Red Shoes, be sure to write,

And I'll look up at your stars every single night.

All too soon it is time to leave.
Ruby feels so sad to say farewell to her
new friend and a city she now loves.

So, with kisses and tears, Babushka Galushka,
Ruby and her well-travelled red shoes say au revoir.

Goodbye, Felix. Goodbye, Gaspar. Goodbye, Paris.

Ruby and Babushka are off to a new city
where there are more family and friends to meet.

See you next time!

Illustrator and artist Kate Knapp is a graduate
of Queensland College of Art. Her Ruby books are
inspired by her family in England, and Babushka
Galushka is based on her English grandmother.
She lived in London for three years in her twenties,
but now lives in Queensland, Australia, where she
runs a design studio, Twigseeds, which produces
greetings cards, stationery, books and homeware.
Ruby Red Shoes Goes to Paris is the
second book in her Ruby Red Shoes series.